Carlo Mulas

Sardinian Folk Tales

Sardinian Folk Tales

by Carlo Mulas

Translated from Italian by David Paul Sommers III

ISBN 978-88-98737-15-4 (eBook)

ISBN 978-88-98737-19-2 (Book)

© Carlo Mulas

Indibooks 2016

Cover image

Giuseppe Biasi

La canzone del pappagallo

(Derivative work)

Storytelling in Sardinia

Up until this last century, storytelling had been very popular in Sardinia.

It isn't that it has completely disappeared, but because of progress, such as the wide use of printing and writing, which have undermined the very roots of this peculiar form of literary communication, it has become more and more scarce.

For centuries oral narration has been much more than a secondary and peripheral phenomenon. As a matter of fact, the telling and listening of tales and legends was of main importance in the life of both the narrators and the listeners.

Narrating was considered a quite serious art.

Whoever excelled in this art gained the *respect* of the people and the attention of the listeners.

The way of telling a tale varied, among other things, depending on the audience, and the geographical and cultural context.

The same story, while still remaining the same in essence and content, could change from time to time to accommodate the tastes of the public, with the idea of catching their attention.

In fact folk tales were therefore a *living* form of art, and narrators would use it to pour out all their experience regarding comprehension of life and human nature, giving also space to their personal artistic expression and their own fantasy.

Stories by the fire-place

In the Sardinian language, legends and folk tales are indicated with the expression *Contos de foghile* and *Contus de forredda* (stories by the fire-place).

Presenting her collection *Fiabe e leggende sarde*, now being a classic of popular literary narrative, Grazia Deledda wrote, '*Contos de fuchile*, with this sweet name that evokes all of the warm serenity of long family evenings spent by the paternal fireplace, is how we call folktales, fables, legends and all those fabulous and wonderful narrations lost in the fog of ages different from ours'.

Cherished for centuries in the culture of the Sardinians and transmitted exclusively by story-telling, Sardinian tales were collected at the end of the Eighteen-hundreds by Sardinian language, culture and traditions researchers: Pier Enea Guarniero, who in 1883-1884 first published *Essays of Sardinian folk tales*, and Francesco Mango, who in 1890 published *Sardinian folk tales*.

The reading of these two anthologies may be quite difficult today, even more so because (in the collection and the transcription of the stories) it was chosen to give priority to the language rather than the actual narration of the story.

In other words, there has been no work in Sardinia similar to the one of the Grimm brothers, nor any kind of attempt to preserve the Sardinian folk and fairy tales, to permit and promote their circulation in written form and a general public knowledge of them.

This book is born with this precise objective: get people, both adults and children, in close contact to Sardinia's most famous folk and fairy tales, which come from its nature and scenarios, and from the historical and social changes that have marked it, including the linguistic and cultural contacts Sardinians have engaged in with other populations in the Mediterranean, from prehistory to the present.

These are, in other words, stories that have similarities with European, Asian and African fables, but at the same time have peculiarities so strong they would not exist in any other place, if not for the Island, such as the Janas and the Nuraghes.

Janas and Nuraghes

The tale that opens this collection is titled *The Queen of the Fairies and the Launeddas Player* (the *launeddas* is an ancient Sardinian breathe instrument made from bamboo) and it is one of my favorite stories, which was told to me in my youth.

It is a wonderful story about love.

Among the main characters there are the Janas.

But, who are the Janas and where do they live?

Janas are Sardinian fairies.

While fairies exist throughout the whole world, Janas only exist in Sardinia.

This word indicates, in the Sardinian language, a category of fairies, usually described as female beings of short stature.

Even though their form and characteristics may vary from place to place, according to popular tradition these creatures would live in the vicinity of prehistoric tombs dug into rocky hills.

These were called, in Sardinian, *Domus de Janas*, meaning house of the fairies.

The Janas are represented as enchanting creatures, often gifted with a sublime voice.

According to some stories passed down through the centuries, they were really beautiful creatures; so beautiful that even today the Sardinian expression *bella cumenti una Jana* (as beautiful as a Jana) defines a very beautiful woman.

In a remote age, the Janas were often in contact with human beings, until human evilness veered them away from society and into a refusal of any contact, hiding in their stone houses.

The Janas were also represented as evil creatures or as dangerous witches and because of this, Sardinian tradition deems it as dangerous entering or going in the proximity of the *Domus*.

The same goes for the Nuraghi (*Nuraghes* or *Nuraxis* in Sardinian), the ancient and mysterious megalithic edifices.

It is said, through a widespread tradition, that these towers of stone have been for many long centuries the houses of monstrous-looking orcs and giants, as suggested by the last fable presented here in this collection, under the title *The orcs and the Nuraghi*.

Snow White and Cinderella in Sardinia

Sardinian oral tradition has preserved the local versions of some of the most famous and widespread fables in the world, but adding such substantial differences to render them absolutely extraordinary.

Among these we also find Snow White and Cinderella.

There are some differences between the tales: Snow White is called *Granadina* and instead of seven dwarves there are thirteen outlaws; while our Cinderella is called *Chiginedda* (or *Cinixera*), who doesn't go to a ball at the palace but to a mass in the church of a Sardinian *bidda* (town).

Actually there is also a Sardinian version of *The Beauty and the Beast*: she is beautiful as always, while he is an orc, a monster or a wild animal, depending on the version.

As in all fables, where wonder and fantasy are blended one into the other, in this collection we have appearances of Kings and Prince Charmings, witches and step-sisters, intelligent servants, witty courtiers and clever women, and of course talking animals and mermaids with magical powers worthy of the One Thousand and One Nights; and we can even find Demons and Devils, with an intact flavor of Inquisition and Spaniardesque.

Although myths and stories about saints are not a part of this collection, they are quite common in Sardinia (contained in another volume).

In this collection there are only those stories characterized by a flavor for narration, in which the main characters struggle with extraordinary events, supernatural creatures, and even more, with enigmatic situations.

The reading of fables is a fun activity and at the same time is a stimulus for our fantasy and imagination, but it must also be considered as an advantageous cultural exercise, great for readers and listeners of all ages.

Carlo Mulas

caralumulas@gmail.com

1. The Queen of the Fairies and the Launeddas Player

Once upon a time the daughter of the King lived in a black castle surrounded by mountains and woods.

The unwed girl spent hours cutting and sewing in a gorgeous room, with needles and scissors in her hands.

When she was tired of working, she would play cards with her ladies in waiting and the women who worked in the castle.

She did not do anything else.

She certainly had a great desire to know the world outside of those enormous glass windows, because she knew with certainty that there was a prince or the son of a king waiting for her out there.

One day, bored from looking out of a window, she wrapped her long blonde hair with a big shawl and followed a path into the woods.

She peacefully walked among violets and cyclamens, breathing a flowery air as full of life as she had ever felt in her life.

Here and there she picked a flower to put it in her hair, loose and as yellow as gold.

And so, walking little by little, she reached a well kept rose garden, one that could not have grown spontaneously, but must have been grown by someone, such was its beauty.

Attracted by that smell, she picked a beautiful rose, as those found solely in fairies' or emperor's gardens.

At first she breathed its perfume, burying her nose in its petals.

She then brought it to her chest and gently caressed it, making sure not to break it.

"What are you doing?" said a manly voice.

"Me?" she answered, opening her eyes and hiding the rose behind her back.

In front of her was a handsome man, with two dark and sad eyes. He was tall and thin with black hair, which was long as was the custom back then.

"Yes, exactly you! Don't you know this is the garden of *Sa Jana Maista*?".

"*Jana Maista*?" echoed the girl.

"Yes, of the Fairy Queen," he explained.

"No, I knew nothing of this. But then again, I did not mean anything bad," she answered looking at him.

So with a severe tone he added, "yes, because I'm the guardian of this rose garden".

After saying this he looked at the girl, who was observing him in amazement, so he finally let out a smile that filled his face. With a quick move he then picked a prettier rose, and gave it to her.

"For you are more beautiful than any fairy," is all he said.

"So, who are you then?" she asked while smelling the flower, which smelled like love.

"My name is Michele and I'm a *launeddas* player. I once lived in a town close to a great pond, where I learned to play this instrument. Ever since I was a child I had a great talent, because I could play it by ear without struggling. As I got older I began gaining experience, playing at parties in the villages and cities, accomplishing great success. This because I had the blessing of making people dance with happiness," he told her all in one breath, while she attentively watched him in silence.

"One morning," continued the sad eyed boy, "I was walking down a path that went through a valley full of rocks with holes in them similar to little ovens. I don't know why, but I felt like playing, so I pulled out of my *launeddas* case the three canes, and started making music under the shade of a tree. Those notes woke the Queen of Fairies, *sa Jana Maista,* up. She had never heard a sweeter melody. Then, I don't know why, I fell asleep. When I woke up I was already in the fairies' kingdom, kidnapped by the Queen who had taken me to play for them. Only then did I realize that those rocks full of holes were in reality *Domus de Janas*".

"Why are you now here in this garden of roses?" she asked.

"It is the spell the queen put upon me: by morning I must guard these roses and by night I must return to their kingdom. You have no idea how much I would like to break this enchantment and live like other mortals!" he sadly said.

With much sadness she asked, "can't anything be done?"

"Of course," he said, hugging her, "you can free me tonight because the moon shall be full and all the fairies shall come out to feast and party".

"Tell me what I must do," she said.

"Wait for me in this rose garden," he said pointing at a beautiful bush, "until the fairies' parade passes through. I will be there too, at the end of the parade on a green horse. Forget about the fairies, but as soon as you see me coming, jump at me and knock me off the horse and hug me as hard as you can, without ever letting me go for any reason upon this Earth: only then I will be free again".

The girl hid among the roses, smelling that magnificent odor.

Moonlight shined on the entire rose garden, while the wind made the leaves and branches move. With courage and without fear she waited for the right moment to do the right thing.

She waited in silence until she heard the noise of people dancing.

The sound of *launeddas* was getting closer quickly, as were the terrible screeches of the fairies.

Upon the sight of those mad dancers, whose faces were white and finger nails were long, she stayed still.

She moved only when she had seen him.

Only then did she leave the thorny bush, and with excellent speed she jumped on him, knocking him to the ground and holding onto him at every moment.

The music had finished.

The *launeddas* player had practically disappeared, wrapped up in the girl's body.

The Queen of the fairies stopped to understand what was going on.

"Where did he go?" she asked the other fairies.

"Over there. Hugged by that woman," yelled one of them.

While she hugged him with all her might, his face pressed firmly into her chest.

At a certain point the girl started to feel something like a fire on her chest, as if the man had been caught by a high fever.

She wouldn't let him go.

Michele's eyes started to *transform*: sadness was going away.

She started to scream from the pain, but the more it hurt her, the more she held him with all her strength, so hard she thought she might be close to dying.

"*Adiosu*, Michele," the Queen of fairies said to stop the fire that was killing both of them.

"Go back to playing for the mortals," she said.

Then, the Queen of fairies and all her company left, disappearing before the sun smiled on the woods, and leaving the two young people exhausted, but alive and happy too.

2. Jaja Zipuledda

Once upon a time there was a man, who had half of a broad bean.

One day he knocked on the door of a house.

A woman opened the door and he asked her, "excuse me, could you do me a favor and keep this broad bean safe for me while I go to mass?".

"Of course," answered the woman, putting it on the table.

A little while later a rooster entered the kitchen and ate the broad bean.

When the mass had finished, the poor man once again knocked on the woman's door to get his broad bean back.

The woman was mortified and had to admit, "I don't have the half of a broad bean anymore because the rooster ate it".

"Well then, either you give me the broad bean or the rooster. Either the half a bean or the rooster".

So the woman gave him the rooster.

After some time, the man went to another house.

He knocked on a door that was opened by a woman and he asked, "excuse me, could you do me the favor and keep this rooster while I go to church?".

"Certainly", answered the woman.

She had a pig, which in turn ate the rooster after the man had left.

After attending church, the man knocked at the door intending to get his rooster back, but the woman told him, "I don't have it anymore. It was eaten by the pig".

"Well then, either you give me the rooster or the pig. Either the rooster or the pig".

So the woman then gave him the pig.

Some time passed and the man went to another house.

"Pardon me, could you please keep this pig while I attend the mass?".

"Certainly," answered the woman who had opened the door. But in this house there was a horse which ate the pig.

When the man got back from the church, the woman had to admit, "the horse ate the pig". And so it was that the man received the horse in exchange.

At another house the man left the horse and went to church.

In that house there were two children that took the horse to drink from a stream. But the horse ran away. When the man got back and asked for the horse, the woman had to sadly report that the animal had run away when her two little girls were taking it to drink some water.

"Well, either the horse or the children. Either the horse or the two little girls!" said the man taking the two little girls, closing them in a bag and leaving, towards another house where an old lady was frying *zipolas* (donuts).

At this time, using a hole in the bag, the two little girls stick out their fingers and yelled, "*Jaja Zipuledda*! *Jaja Zipuledda*!".

In fact, the old woman was really *sa jaja*, or grandmother, who, as soon as she heard her grandchildren's voices was able to let the two little girls out, filling the bag instead with two mad dogs.

So, the man returned to pick up the bag.

He carried it upon his head and walked away, headed toward his home, happy at the thought of getting a nice meal with those two girls.

When he got home, he opened his sack from which the two mad dogs came out and bit into his neck, killing him.

3. From the Earth to the Sky

Once upon a time a king had a gorgeous canary.

He loved it so much he even put a servant in charge of feeding it, taking care of it and making sure it did not escape.

One pleasant morning, the servant did not notice that he had left the little cage door open, and the canary had taken off and flown away.

That man was caught by the deepest desperation, as he knew the king would have him punished, because of the pain of the loss of his so loved canary.

When the king found out what had happened, the king ordered the servant to leave the castle forever.

The man, his desperation growing by the minute, promised the king that such a shortcoming would not be repeated.

This said, he started to cry, kneeling at the feet of the king and hoping to be forgiven, as his copious family would risk famine and death for his mistake.

The king, moved by compassion, then told the man in a calm voice, "all right. But listen to me carefully. I will ask you two questions to which you will have to give two answers. If you answer correctly, you will remain in my castle. Otherwise I will expel you with shame".

"Please speak, Majesty", answered the servant, "I am ready".

"By tomorrow you must tell me what the distance between the earth and the sky is and how many stones it took to build my castle".

The servant listened carefully.

He remained silent and right after promised that the next day he would answer the two questions, even though he was conscious of the fact he did not know the answers.

He left the royal residence in desperation with an even greater explosion of tears.

Outside the palace he encountered a friend of his, who upon seeing him crying in such a manner, asked him the reason of so many tears.

The servant told him of what had happened and told his friend of the two incredible questions.

"This is the cause of all this desperation?" asked his smiling friend, who right after added, "the answer, in fact, is quite easy to find and I will immediately show you. First, take a ball of wool, the biggest you can find, and explain to the king that it is the distance that separates the earth from the sky. As for the stones instead, go ahead and tell him there are two million! And if he has the courage to reply or make any kind of observation, well, tell him he can go measure the distance and he can go count the stones!".

The servant thanked his friend and got back home with some hope.

The next day he woke up early and presented himself at the king's court.

Then the king asked him, "so, have you been able to find the answers to the two dilemmas I proposed to you yesterday?".

"Of course, Majesty. As to your first question", said the servant showing the big ball of wool, "the distance that there is from the earth to the sky is equal to the length of this ball".

The king replied, "no, that is not true. That is not the answer".

The servant, in a placid and determined manner, remarked, "then you can measure it and see if I am right or wrong".

The king remained silent, because he did not know how to reply to the determined statement of the servant. And so, with a certain tone of annoyance, he asked once more, "and as regards to the number of stones it took to build my castle, what will you tell me now?".

"Sire, your palace is made up of exactly two million of stones".

"Give me a break," replied the king, "that is not true".

"Yes, it is true," remarked the servant once more. "Actually, it is very true, and if you don't believe me, you can count them yourself and, in doing so, will see that I have told you the truth".

The king, amazed by the strength of spirit and of the courage of the servant, not only kept him in his castle, but also gave him a large sum of money, which the man gladly split with his friend who had helped him get out of the huge problematic situation.

4. Once Upon a Time

Once upon a time there was a very rich merchant that desired to give his shop away. And so he made a proclamation: he would give his shop to whomever had the ability of telling him a story without saying 'once upon a time', but if the teller made the mistake of saying 'once upon a time', the teller would have to give something in return!

There were also three brothers whose father had recently died leaving them in heredity a horse, a saddle and some reins. The oldest got the reins, the second oldest one the saddle and the youngest the horse.

When the three heard that the merchant had spread the news regarding his intentions to give away his shop, the oldest of the three said, "I really want to go tell him a story".

"All right, but be careful not to say *once upon a time*", the other two reminded him.

"Why, of course I will be careful".

Said so he took the reins and went to see the merchant.

"Pardon me. Are you by any chance the merchant that would like to hear a story without the words *once upon a time?*".

"Yes, I am. So, come on and begin".

"*Once upon a time…*".

"Stop there," said the merchant, taking the reins away from him.

The oldest of the brothers sadly left.

Once back home, the other two asked him how it had gone.

He replied that not only had he not obtained the shop, but had also lost the reins.

"What are you saying? *Tontu* (stupid)," said the second of the brothers, who promptly added, "now I will go and you will see me win".

So he took the saddle and went to the shop and asked, "pardon me, are you by any chance the merchant that would like to hear a story without the words *once upon a time?*".

"Yes, I am. So, come on, begin".

"*Once upon a time…*".

"Stop here," he said taking the saddle away.

The second of the brothers sadly left.

Once he had returned home, the other two asked him how it had gone.

He answered that not only had he not obtained the shop, but had also lost the saddle.

"I will go," said the youngest of the three after a bit, "and we will see if he is able to beat me too".

After this he took his horse, entered the shop and asked, "pardon me, are you by any chance the merchant that would like to hear a story without the words *once upon a time?*".

"Yes, I am. So, come on in and begin".

"After my mother had given birth to me, she sent me to buy some matches, but with that money I bought myself a melon.

Once I cut it open, I found a note inside it where there was written: *Get out, you merchant, for the shop is mine"*.

At this point the merchant left, leaving him with the whole shop, the saddle and the reins.

The youngest of the three returned home, so very happy to tell the brothers he had won the shop and would share it equally with them.

It was for this reason that the three lived forever in tranquility.

5. Granadina and the Thirteen Outlaws (Snow White in Sardinia)

Once upon a time there lived a husband with his beautiful wife.

The two did not have any children.

The woman, considered by many to be *una bruscia* (a witch), had a magical mirror, to which she would ask every day, "my round mirror, if not I, what other beauty is there in this world?".

"None other" the mirror would answer.

One day the woman got pregnant and nine months later she had a beautiful baby like none other on this Earth. So it went that, after the birth, the woman went up to the mirror and asked, "my round mirror, if not I, what other beauty is there in this world?".

"Granadina" answered the mirror.

Granadina was the name of the such beautiful child; a child so beautiful, even more than her mother, that the mother could not bear the fact her daughter was better than her.

Every time she asked the mirror who the most beautiful was, it gave her Granadina's name.

One day she decided to summon her most loyal servant, and told him without hesitation, "listen carefully, because you will have to obey my order without hesitation. In the case you refuse to obey, then I will have you killed".

"What can I do for you, my lady?" asked the petrified servant.

"You must kill Granadina," said the woman, with a severe and determined tone.

"And how?" asked the servant.

"Tell her you'll take her for a ride in the carriage. Once you're far away in the country, far away from any eyes and ears, you will kill her".

"As you order, but…" he went on.

"Wait!" said the woman, who promptly added, "to prove the success of her death you must bring me back a finger and a small bottle of her blood. Now what were you saying?".

"How am I going to convince her to come with me? She is now older than eight and certainly not stupid. And she knows, my lady, that you are jealous of her beauty".

"I don't care. That is up to you. Either she dies, or you will die!" she finished off sending the servant away.

And so the man prepared the carriage and convinced the little girl to go with him.

Once the parents' palace was far and out of sight and the vegetation surrounded them, Granandina looked at the man and asked him, "my mother asked you to kill me, didn't she? Then kill me and let's get it over with!".

"No," answered the servant, who immediately added, "we are only taking a ride".

They got in the proximity of a forest, and the man had the girl get out of the carriage.

Looking all around, the girl said vehemently, "go ahead! Kill me, so I know".

But the man appeared to hesitate.

So she asked again, "why don't you to fulfil the desire of my mother? Why don't you get it over with and fulfil my mother's wish?".

The man looked into the eyes of the girl *bella cumenti una jana* and said, "I don't have the courage!". And so, pulling out an axe and a glass bottle from his bag, he added, "let's do this: put your smallest finger on this stone so I can cut it off and put the blood coming out into this bottle. In this way your mother will think you are dead and will find her peace".

Without hesitating, Granadina put her pinky on the stone.

With a swift sharp cut the pinky was off, rapidly filling the small bottle, redder and redder with blood. He medicated her hand with care, then told her, while caressing her hair, "stay here, safe. Down that path is *unu padenti cracu* (a forest) where you can hide. I will bring you food every day. But you must be careful".

"All right," replied the little girl, grasping tight her hand in pain.

She watched as the servant left on the carriage with her pinky and some of her red blood.

Once back at the palace, the woman asked the man if he had fulfilled his duty.

"Of course, my lady. Your order has been fulfilled. As proof of the girl's death I have brought you her pinky and the bottle with her blood. Look here".

"Splendid! You have done well. For this your life is safe. And now leave".

Joyful with the terrible news, the woman immediately ran to her mirror and, without wasting any second, asked, "my round mirror, if not I, what other beauty is there in this world?".

"Granadina", answered the magical mirror.

"What? Granadina?" she blabbered amazed, "but she is dead! How is it possible that the mirror still says she's the most beautiful? Maybe the servant has tricked me! In that case I will find her and she will not have a chance".

Time passed.

The servant, as promised, brought the girl food every day.

It was so that another eight years had passed.

The girl had grown older, keeping her beauty intact: her face white as snow and her cheeks red as the seeds of *sa mela granada*, or pomegranate, which her name came from.

One day Granadina felt like taking a walk in the woods.

She was tired of staying in the hut, so she went for a walk.

Walking a long way she lost her way back and began wandering through the thick woods, until she saw a house.

She got closer, walking ever quicker, to that house, whose chimney had a friendly smoke escaping.

She knocked on the door but nobody answered or opened it.

She turned its knob, the door opened and she went in.

In the room there was a long table, with thirteen places set: thirteen plates, thirteen sandwiches and thirteen bottles. A joyful fire burned in the kitchen, and in it there was a skewer with a large piece of meat roasting.

Intrigued, she began to wander about the house but found no one.

Even the large bedroom, with thirteen beds, was empty.

So she began to clean and put the house in order, because it was dirty and untidy.

Because she had not eaten, she decided to cut a piece of meat from the spit.

Then she took a piece of bread from every sandwich on the table and a drop of wine from each of the bottles.

Once her belly was full, she got very sleepy and crawled under one of the beds.

The thirteen men arrived back home.

They were a band of notorious bandits who lived in the house.

Upon entering, they found everything clean and the food ready. But everything was not well, because each of their place settings lacked a little bit of wine and a piece of bread from each of their meals.

"Someone has broken into our house," said one.

"There must be some mischievous *bird*," said a second.

"We must get him!" said another.

"Tomorrow, someone must remain on guard," added a fourth.

"I'll stay!" said another one.

They ate and went to bed, unaware of the presence of the girl lying under one of their beds.

The next day they left all but one that stood out the door, believing that the thief bird came from the forest.

Granadina woke up and did exactly what she had done the day before.

The bandits returned home and saw that everything was clean and a bit of food and a bit of wine was missing.

"*Ta tontu chi ses!* You're incompetent!" said the first turning to the keeper.

"Is this what you call keeping watch!?" said another.

"You have been cheated like a fool!" was the comment of the other cronies.

"Tomorrow I'll stay," was the conclusion of one of the gang.

The next day the same thing happened as the previous days.

"*Ta tontu chi ses!*" said the first.

"But I did not see anyone enter. I was out the door all day but no-one showed up, neither man nor animal," was the response of the bandit who had been on guard.

"So there must be someone in the house", added a third.

"Let's do this, tomorrow I'll stay," said the older and most experienced of the band.

And so, unlike the others, the expert outlaws decided to stay at home, not outside.

Suddenly, he saw Granadina come out from under one of the beds and was amazed by her beauty.

"*No mi bocis po praxeri!* Please do not kill me," said the girl with red cheeks and white face.

The man looked at her and she began to tell him the whole story.

"Do not worry," the bandit assured her.

Then, stroking her black hair, he said, "you will be treated as a sister. I can assure you, I am the oldest and also the wisest, and all the others give it to me straight. For the moment, do what you do every day. However, do not leave this house because your mother could see you and kill you without mercy. In fact, I think she may know that you're still alive".

The girl put the house in order and prepared the meat, then ate and laid down under one of the beds.

"I caught the *bird*. It was inside as assumed," the bandit told the rest of the old gang. Then, taking a big crucifix that was hanging from one of the white walls, he said to them, "now swear sacred on this image of Christ on the cross that you will obey what I'm about to tell you".

"*Bandabeni!* Okay!" answered the other twelve as one, kissing the crucifix.

"No *bird* it is, but a nice girl," the oldest announced to the amazement of his cronies, to whom he recounted word for word the whole story. Then, soon after, he added, "now you have sworn on this crucifix that you will treat her like a sister, and not even hurt a hair on her body".

"Okay," replied the men, kissing the cross vigorously.

The leader called the girl, who promptly walked out of the bedroom.

The bandits, upon seeing her, were fascinated by so much beauty, so much so that all together they sighed: "*Ermosa! Galana!* (Wonderful!)".

It was easy to love their new sister, who was so beautiful as good.

To express their feelings, the bandits brought her fine clothes and precious jewels, and accommodated her needs and wishes of any fashion.

When the servant brought food to the girl, he did not find her.

Thinking that she had been torn up and killed by some herd of wild animals, he wept and prayed for her soul.

A while later the bandits decided to take Granadina to one of the biggest country festivals of the island.

"Put on and wear your best clothes for *sa festa manna* (the big and great party). We will go now but we'll come back to get you later with the horses".

The girl began to dress.

Because she was happy she opened all the windows and looked out over the countryside to breathe the air of celebration on this joyful day.

Just then, an old woman, who was selling shoes embroidered with gold, came up to the house, calling the beautiful maiden.

"*Prenda de coru* (take with heart)," she said, "try on these golden shoes: in this way you will be the most beautiful at the party".

The girl, radiant and happy, putting aside all suspicion, approached the old woman, thinking it was one of many traders that the holidays bring hopelessly behind, as *carapigna* (shaved ice with lemon) sellers of Aritzo and the nougat sellers of Tonara, or as orange traders of Milis and those of *lissa* (mullet) coming from Cabras.

Then, she took a golden shoe and put it on her foot.

For a moment she gasped.

With all her strength she put the other one on, then fell unconscious to the ground.

The old woman, who was none other than the mother in disguise, left in a hurry, leaving Granadina motionless on the cold ground.

In this way the thirteen bandits found her when they went to take her to the big party.

The elder approached the lifeless body, and without hesitation gave the sad confirmation to other men.

Granadina was dead.

Everyone began to cry and, without waiting any longer, they began to build a wooden coffin, with a glass cover.

Once the body of Granadina, which was turning always whiter, was lying on the bottom they closed the coffin with the glass cover and stood in the doorway of their home.

One day, the king's son passed in front of the bandit's home.

The prince, upon seeing the girl in the coffin, fell in love at once.

So he put the coffin into his carriage and took her to the palace.

He called a servant and ordered him to carry the coffin to his room and did not tell anyone, not even the king and queen.

He would go out just to eat, because he spent all his time at the side of the dead girl.

The queen, intrigued by the behavior of her son, thought of going to peek into his room to understand what secret he was keeping.

She got the key and took advantage of a moment of absence of the young prince to sneak inside.

To her greatest amazement her eyes fell upon the gorgeous girl lying down.

Noting the golden shoes on her feet, she took one off so that she could admire it closer.

Granadina took a breath.

Then she took the other shoe off.

The girl returned to life, but continued to sleep.

Just then, the prince returned to his room.

"Mother, why did you come and open the door?".

"I wanted to see why you left your room so rarely. Now I get it".

Then she showed the prince the shoes and the girl's bare feet, telling him to put his ear to her heart, which suddenly was beating again.

"I want you to marry her," added the queen.

So it was that the marriage was arranged between the happiness and joy of the couple, their loved ones and the people of the kingdom.

Even the bandits were invited to the party, because they had treated the princess with love, who certainly did not forget her brothers, who, after marriage, remained forever in the castle to live.

6. The Devil and the Fisherman

Once upon a time a fisherman from Cabras roamed the sea, but he was persecuted by bad luck.

Anywhere he threw his nets he never caught anything.

As a consequence he was very poor, and he had recently lost his wife.

In addition to this he also had a daughter.

One day as he prepared to go to throw his nets somewhere, he met a guy who he had never seen before.

It was the devil himself, who stopped him and said: "look, you're poor and unfortunate, and will never catch anything. If you give me your daughter, every time you go out in the boat you shall pull in so many fish that you will become rich. What do you say?".

"What do I have to do?" asked the fisherman, without any hesitation.

"Well, it is enough that you do what I tell you. I will come to your house at midnight. When I knock on the door it is important that your daughter opens it. That's all".

"All right," said the fisherman.

That day he fished many fish as it had never happened before.

Happily he went to the market to sell a part of the catch.

Then he came home and cooked for himself and his daughter a lot of fish.

With their bellies full at last, they went to bed.

At midnight there was a knock at the door.

The fisherman ordered his daughter to open it.

Before turning the handle, she made the sign of the cross across her chest.

She opened the door and saw no one.

Then she went to her father to tell him that she had opened the door but had not found anyone outside.

"All right, back to sleep," says the fisherman.

The next night the devil came at the same time.

He knocked on the door, and the girl made the sign of the cross and then opened the door once more and once more didn't see anyone.

The next morning the devil, angry because he could not take her soul, complained to the fisherman, who asked, "what should I do?".

"Cut her hand off," replied the devil.

Later that night at midnight he punctually showed up at the door and knocked, but the girl made the sign of the cross with her other hand which had not been cut off.

Then the devil, increasingly angry, decided to drown the fisherman.

The girl, poor and without a hand, did not know how she was going to take care of herself.

She decided to beg on the street.

This is how she took up asking for charity on the road.

This continued until an old couple had compassion for her, seeing her in such a state, and took her back to their house.

They were rich and had a son.

After a bit of time the young man fell in love with the fisherman's daughter and decided to marry her against the wishes of his mother, who was very much against the wedding.

A year after the wedding the girl gave birth to healthy and strong twins.

But as fate would have it, war started and the father of the twins went off to war.

Before leaving, the man told his mother that she was to take good care of his wife and children. She promised, but as soon as her son left, she called a servant and ordered him to kill the woman and her two children.

The servant had always been faithful, but took the family to the country because he could not slaughter them.

So the three hid in a secret house where, every day, the servant would bring them food.

When the war ended, the husband came home and asked his mother for news of his wife and children. The woman, then, lied and said, "she's left you with the children who-knows-where".

The man was sad and desperate, and he constantly thought about his wife.

It was another two years.

One day he decided to go hunting in the country.

Suddenly a powerful storm started, which prompted him to seek shelter in a house not far but hidden in the green.

It was the house where, a few years ago, his wife and children had hidden, but he did not know that.

"Dear lady," he said to the woman, without recognizing her, "could I ask you the favor of staying in your house tonight?".

"Sure," she replied recognizing her husband.

The man came in and, seeing the two brats, said to himself, "my children would be the same age as these children".

Once the man had fallen asleep, the woman told the children, "go to the man and tell him: Daddy, Daddy".

The man woke up and said, "so you are my own children!".

Then, turning to the two children, he added, "call your mother!".

The woman stood in front of her husband, who immediately asked, "why did you run away?".

"My dear, I did not run away. You must know that your mother decided to kill me and your children. This order was given to the most faithful of servants who, because of his good nature, could not do that act of barbarity. So he brought me to this house in the country and since then brings us something to eat every single day".

So it was that the man went back home, drove his mother away, and remained there forever with his wife, children and the servant.

7. The Orc and the Princess with the Cat-Face

There once were two wives who were very fond of each other and always went out together.

One day, while out for a walk, they passed near a vegetable garden.

One of the two, who was pregnant, saw a mushroom and said to the other, "My Mistress, we must enter the garden, because I saw a beautiful mushroom and I really want it."

"All right", said the other, "we should enter right away and take advantage of this moment while there is no one watching".

The two women entered stealthily, approaching the mushroom with measured slow step.

They tried to pick it but they could not get it to come out of the ground.

They pulled and pulled again, but the mushroom would not come out of the ground, until, at the brink of their strength and red from the strain, the women tried one last time, putting all their strength in the effort into pulling it out.

At this point, an orc suddenly materialized, who said to the women, "tell you what, I'll give you the mushroom, because you want it so much, but on one condition: when the child you are carrying is four years old, she will become mine and you will have to bring her here and give her to me".

The woman, whose desire for the mushroom was stronger than anything else, agreed.

Some time later she gave birth to a beautiful little girl who she named Maria.

She had white and pink skin, and her hair was like gold.

The more she grew, the more beautiful she became.

When Maria turned four years of age, her mother remembered the promise she had made to the orc, and took her to him in the place where she had pocketed the mushroom.

The orc immediately fell in love.

"You will be my partner", he said.

The mother left Maria alone to live with the ogre.

He lived in a beautiful palace and the girl immediately became the mistress of the palace.

The orc, for his part, loved her very much, but was also very jealous of her.

For this reason, the ogre would never let her go out and kept the door locked at all times.

When he would come home to his beautiful house, he would call for Maria and say, *"mela mia de àpiu, ghetamì is pilus chi mi nci àrtziu"* (my little apple, throw down your hair so I may climb it).

With this said she would throw down her long golden hair and he would enter the building through the window, which she often looked out of.

Time passed and Maria finally became eighteen.

As she grew older she became more and more beautiful.

One day while she was looking out of the window she saw a handsome young man sitting in a carriage on the road, looking at her enchanted, and she immediately fell in love.

It was a prince who upon seeing her, sighed with determination, "I want to marry that girl".

So it was that the prince began to walk past the orc's building every single day.

One day, while she was looking for something in a drawer, Maria found three balls of wool.

"What good are these balls?" she asked the orc.

"These balls are very helpful and they have extraordinary powers. They help you when you are being chased and prevent those who are chasing you to catch you. In fact, when you throw the first one it will turn into a sea of water, the second into a sea of fire, and the third into a sea of thorns", said the orc to the girl, revealing the powers of the three balls.

As soon as she heard these words, Maria took possession of them.

The orc, in fact, did not know that she was planning to run away with the prince, who passed in front of her window with his carriage every day.

The two had agreed and had made a plan: he would have to bring a long wooden ladder and put it under her window, from which she was supposed to climb down.

On the appointed day the prince showed up at the foot of the window with a smooth wooden ladder that he worked to put securely on the windowsill.

Maria, without any difficulty, and bringing the balls with her, climbed down the ladder and immediately slipped inside the carriage with the prince.

A moment later, the carriage left in a hurry.

The orc, as usual, came home and called to young Maria to receive the long braid of hair.

He called and called but no one answered.

He entered the house and called again.

Nothing.

He went up to her room but it was empty.

From the open window he saw a carriage pulling away in a hurry.

He looked inside the carriage and saw Maria in the company of the prince.

Without hesitating a moment, he set off in pursuit of the two lovers.

But as soon as she saw that he was following them, she took the first of the balls and threw it.

A sea of water met the orc, but by opening his mouth, he managed to drink all the water in one gulp.

Without fear, Maria threw another ball which turned into a sea of fire, but the orc was able to put it out by spitting all the water he had just swallowed a moment ago.

Fearing nothing, she threw the last ball at him from which a sea of thorns came out.

The orc was now a prisoner.

Realizing that he did not have a way out, he called Maria and said, "look at me one last time".

The girl turned and he said to her: "May your face become like one of a cat."

And so it did.

Finally they arrived at the prince's castle and everyone was struck by the girl with the cat face.

The queen, with some disdain, asked her son, "do you really want to marry this monstrosity?".

"Mother, when I kidnapped her she had a beautiful face, even more beautiful than yours," replied the prince.

But the queen wanted nothing to do with the woman with a face like that of a cat.

She was both afraid and disgusted.

The wedding was postponed.

So it was the prince decided to lock her in a room and not let her out again.

The girl suffered and felt unhappy, because during the long period spent with the orc she had never been hurt.

Her dreams were shattered but she did not lose heart.

Finally one day the king ordered all daughters-in-law to weave curtains and give them to him. Even Maria was asked to participate.

The king would choose the best woven one.

So what did Maria do?

Well, desperate, she sent a servant to the orc to tell him that the king had commanded all the daughters-in-law to give him woven curtains and she did not know how to do this. So it was that the orc sent beautiful curtains to Maria. On the evening of the presentation, Maria got dressed and went to the reception room.

The sisters-in-law looked at each other and laughed and whispered sarcastically, "so what do you think cat face did?".

The presentation began.

Among all the curtains viewed, the king especially loved those made by Maria, to whom he gave many compliments, while to the others he didn't say a word.

The women were jealous and hated the girl even more than before.

Once the presentation was over, each one returned to her own room.

The next morning Maria took courage and sent the servant to talk to the orc once more.

She asked the orc to send her a chest that contained water to remove the cat skin from her face and return it to the way it was before.

So it happened that the orc made her have a beautiful chest with special water and soaps.

With these Maria washed.

The cat face slowly disappeared.

She looked in the mirror, where she finally saw her true face, white and pink.

It was then that the prince married her and they decided to have the orc to stay with them at the castle.

8. Chiginera (The Sardinian Cinderella)

There was once a man who had a wife and three daughters.

One day his wife died, leaving her husband alone with the three girls.

The two older daughters seemed more clever than the younger one, who gave the impression of being a little naive and foolish.

She usually did the domestic tasks and took care of the kitchen.

The father and sisters called her Chiginera, because, in fact, she was always dirty of *chigina* (ash).

The death of the mother forced the man to change jobs and become a trader.

He would often go down to the city to buy the merchandise to sell in his shop.

Before leaving, he would always ask his daughters if they wished him to bring them a gift.

One day, to this question, the two older daughters said they wanted two beautiful and rare skirts, the kind that would arouse the envy of all the other girls in the village during the great festival to be held shortly thereafter.

"Give my regards to *su puzone medianu* (the bird in the middle), who is a bird jumping from branch to branch," said Chiginera however, starting her sisters into a fit of laughter.

So it was that the father went on his journey.

At one point, not too far from the woods, he saw a bird approaching him, to which he said, "hey, *su puzone medianu*, greetings from my daughter".

"Many thanks," replied the bird and, dropping a nut onto the hand of man, he added, "give her this from me".

The trader put the walnut into his haversack and continued on his journey to the city.

After finishing his business and having purchased two beautiful skirts for the girls, he began his journey home.

As soon as he opened the door, he was immediately asked for the gifts.

"Look! With these two skirts, you two will be the most elegant in the country," said the man showing their skirts.

"Did the bird send Chiginera something?" asked the sisters.

"*Eja* (yes)," said the man, laughing, "he sent a nut."

"*Ta tonta* (How stupid)! She seems like a dog looking for food! She does not care about clothes! She could put a rag on and be happy!" said the oldest one provoking the laughter of the second.

"Chiginera, come here," cried the father, who immediately added, "*to' piga* (here), this walnut was given to me by *su puzone medianu* for you".

"*Gràtzias Babbu*! (thank you father)," said the young girl, returning to sit beside *sa tziminera* (the fireplace), where she hid the nut she had received as a gift.

Some time after the father had to go back down into the city to do more shopping.

"What can I bring you from the city?" he asked his three daughters.

"*Unu mucadore*," said the first.

"I want a handkerchief too," said the second.

"Give my regards to *su puzone medianu*: he may have something else for me," said Chiginera.

The father went on his journey.

Not too far from the woods, he saw the bird approaching him.

"*Su puzone medianu*, greetings from my daughter!" he said.

"Thank you!" the bird said in turn and dropped an almond on the hand of the man, adding, "give her this from me."

The trader pocketed the almond and continued his journey.

After getting all the business done and having purchased two beautiful handkerchiefs for his older daughters, he returned home.

"What did you bring?" said the oldest.

"Here are your handkerchiefs: there are none more beautiful in the world!" said the man showing his daughters their colorful gifts.

"What did the bird give Chiginera this time?".

"*Méndula*," said the father extracting the almond and calling the youngest daughter who, after thanking him, took the almond and returned to the fireplace.

The day of the great festival, *sa festa manna*, came.

The older sisters dressed up in their new clothes and went out to the first Mass in the festively decorated village church.

The two older sisters laughed heartily seeing the youngest dressed in rags.

As soon as the two oldest sisters had closed the door, Chiginera went to the fireplace.

She opened the nut: a team of servants came out of it.

She then opened the almond: the most beautiful party dresses that had ever been seen and a pair of fantastic silver shoes came out of it.

Once the servants had the girl dressed as a princess, they also left the house to go to the solemn Mass.

In the church *su Donnichellu*, namely the Crown Prince, and son of *su Giùighe,* the King, was also present.

The young man, as soon as he saw Chiginera dressed as a princess, fell madly in love.

But the girl, for fear of being recognized by the sisters, did not stay after the mass.

As soon as the ceremony was over, she ran away in a hurry.

As she was leaving, she lost one of the silver shoes that was picked up by the Prince, who looked for the girl but could not find her.

He decided to launch the following notice, "the young woman, who during the Mass lost the silver shoe, would marry the prince and would become princess".

All the women of the village waited for their turn to try on the shoe.

The prince himself went door to door with shoe in hand to search for his future princess.

At the home of Chiginera, he asked the two older sisters if, apart from them, there was any other girl: might she be a servant or cook.

It wasn't important.

"There's our sister," said the oldest.

"But it can not be her, she never leaves the house and if she does it is in hideous garments," added the other.

"It will be a waste of time for your majesty, but if you want to see her, she will be in the kitchen," said the oldest, indicating the staircase leading to the kitchen, where the two older sisters did not enter for fear of getting their clothes and hair dirty.

The future king went into the kitchen where he saw Chiginera still dressed like a princess, with a single silver shoe on her foot. Approaching with care, he put the other shoe on her and without saying anything to her sisters left.

The next day, the second day of the great feast, the sisters dressed themselves and they went out to the morning mass.

Even Chiginera, dressed up by the servants from the nut in her clothes from the almond, left to go to church with a bunch of roses.

There she met her sisters, who did not recognize her.

"If you gave us a flower each, you will make two friends," said the oldest.

"All right, I will give you each a flower, but I will also give you a slap each," said Chiginera.

"As you wish, as long as nobody is looking," said one of the sisters.

Chiginera gave them two slaps and two roses.

Then, as soon as the priest had finished saying Mass, she ran back to the house, where she took off her dress and silver shoes.

After a bit of time even the sisters got back who, seeing their father, told him that they had received the flowers from the prettiest girl and best dressed that they had ever seen.

"Yes, but to have the roses, you each also received a slap!" said Chiginera.

The sisters were petrified and muted.

Chiginera then invited her father to go to the kitchen where she had prepared a great lunch.

The sisters laughed out loud and suggested to their father not to go.

He on the other hand decided to follow the youngest daughter.

Amazed, upon entering the kitchen, he saw a large number of servants and cooks all busy preparing the finest lunch he had ever seen.

The table was laid with silver cutlery and crystal glasses.

The Prince was also sitting.

He told Chiginera's father that he found the owner of the silver shoe and it was Chiginera, who would become his wife.

After eating they went to the castle of the king and Chiginera did not want to see her sisters ever again.

So it was that she married the young prince, who was none other than *su puzone medianu*, changed by a spell to jump from branch to branch until the love of Chiginera had freed him.

9. The Orc's Rose

There was once a merchant who had three daughters.

Because he had to leave on business, he asked his daughters what they wanted him to bring them back from the trip.

The oldest one asked for a dress, the second one asked for a hat, while the third one asked for a rose.

The father left and went to the city where he found all the goods he needed for his shop.

After he had finished his purchases, he bought the dress and hat, but he could not buy the rose for the youngest.

Feeling miserable, he started on the way back home, when, at some point, passing in front of a garden, he saw a beautiful rose.

He looked around and, believing that there was nobody around, sneaked into the rose garden and picked the beautiful rose.

Suddenly a very large orc, *unu Pundu mannu,* came out.

He was halfway between a man and a beast.

In a very nasty tone he asked the shopkeeper, "why would you take one of my roses?".

"I took it because I wanted to give it as a gift to my daughter, to whom I had promised one when I returned from my business trip. Unfortunately, at the market I did not find any. So, seeing this garden that seemed abandoned, I decided to go in and pick the most beautiful rose".

"All right, I'll give it to you, but on one condition," said the monster.

"What do you want?" asked the merchant.

"You must bring me your daughter," replied the orc.

"Okay," said the merchant, who wanted to keep his promise to his daughter, so he took the rose and returned home.

On his return, the daughters asked him at once if he had remembered to bring them the gifts he had promised.

"Sure," replied the father, handing the dress to the first, the hat to the second and the stolen rose to the third.

Right after this he told the third daughter, "as you can see I have brought you the rose, but I need you to come with me tomorrow," and the daughter agreed.

The next morning the father and daughter made their way toward the orc's garden.

Once they were near the garden, the man left, telling his daughter to go into the orc's building and went away.

The young woman was very happy in her new home, because she was served and catered to by the servants.

She was also happy because the orc *fiat lègiu, ma de coru bonu:* ugly outside but nice and beautiful inside.

She passed three months like this until one day the young woman felt sad and cried for a long time.

The orc, who was worried, asked her what was wrong and if she needed something.

The girl then told him she had seen her father in a dream.

He was very ill, and she now feared for his health.

The orc asked her, "would you like to visit him?".

"Yes," she replied.

"So go, but do not stay for more than eight days, or else I will die," said the orc.

"I swear. I will not stay more than eight days," replied the girl.

Accompanied by a servant, the young woman left the palace and went back to her father's house.

The man was very ill.

In the eight days that she stayed the father improved. But her time ran out and she had to leave to keep her word.

However her sisters convinced her to stay two extra days.

She then left for the orc's palace.

When she got there the owner was dead, as he had told her.

The girl then fell in desperation, screaming and crying, until the orc, suddenly began to breathe and move again.

However he was not a monster anymore, but a handsome young man.

In fact, he was a prince, victim of a spell.

Looking at the girl, he said: "My spell has been broken. We will now write to your father and ask him to come here."

When her father came to the palace, the two were married.

10. The Devil and Condemned Souls

There was once a poor man who had a wife and three daughters.

Every day he went into the forest to fetch wood.

One morning while he was cutting a tree he heard footsteps.

He turned and saw a well-dressed gentleman who immediately spoke to him, saying, "good man, what are you doing?".

"Don't you see? I am gathering up a bit of wood to make fire to heat my family".

"May I lend you a hand?".

"Until I die, I can use some help".

"Do you have a large family?" the distinguished gentleman asked the poor man while helping him gather firewood.

"I have three daughters".

"Well, now I'm helping you gather firewood, but I could help you in a much greater manner, possibly by marrying one of your three daughters".

"One of my daughters? But they are so poor!" exclaimed the surprised woodcutter.

At that point, the gentleman grabbed a whole large branch and, in a matter of moments, cut it off the tree and into pieces without any strain, and then gave it to the poor man.

"Tomorrow we will meet again and then you can give me an answer".

"Yes, certainly," said the poor man to the gentleman.

So, talking to himself, he said, "this must surely be the Devil. If not, how could he ever cut that huge branch up so quickly and effortlessly?".

So it was, deep in thought, he returned home and told his daughters what had happened.

"No, Dad, I don't want to be the bride," said the oldest.

"No, no, me neither," said the second.

"I will marry him," said the youngest, who immediately added, "in this way I shall be a lady in my own house".

The next morning, before leaving, the father asked his daughter, "do you really want to marry him?".

"Yes, I do," she said without hesitation.

As soon as he entered the forest the gentleman met him and without greeting him in any other way said, "so? Is there by any chance any of your three daughters who will marry me?".

"Yes, the youngest".

"Very well. Take this envelope of money. Tomorrow I will come to your home," said the gentleman taking his leave.

Once he had returned home, the man organized everything for the wedding.

On the day the two were married, they immediately left to go live in his house.

The girl's mother, before letting her go, gave her a small dog to keep her company.

The dog and young bride went to the new home with the gentleman.

Once outside the house, the husband told his wife, giving her the keys, "from this moment on you are the master of this all and with these keys you can open all the rooms inside, except for one".

Without telling her why, he showed her around the large house and then took his leave.

"I have to find out why he did not want to give me the key to that room," said the bride to herself, her curiosity growing even stronger noticing her husband would not show himself from mid-day to midnight.

She had tried looking for him many times, but in vain every time.

"I have to find out why he did not want to give me the key to that room," she kept repeating to herself, "and understand why I never see him during the day. Something is not right".

One day, thanks to the instinct of her dog, she managed to find the so desired key.

And so she went towards the mysterious door with the key, put it in the lock and opened the heavy wooden door.

What a sad spectacle presented itself before her eyes!

The room, in fact, was filled with the souls of dead women.

The girl, frightened, found the courage to approach the souls and asked, "who are you?".

"We are condemned souls who are serving their sentence".

"I," said a miller woman, "used to steal a measure of wheat from every poor person who came to me at the mill to measure it".

"I," said another, "would swear all the time".

The third, on the other hand, admitted, "I killed my husband".

One after the other, they all described to the girl why they were serving their sentences. Then, in chorus, they asked the girl, "who are you?".

"I am the lady of the house, the one who lives in this house with her groom, the master".

"Poor child! Do you not know that you're married to the Devil himself?".

"What could I do about it?".

"Do not worry. We can help you find a way to live far away from him".

"How?".

"Write a letter and pretend to have received it from your mother. Write that your mother is ill, misses you and desires to see you again soon. Give it to your husband and ask him to take you straight home to your parents. Once you are there, get a rooster for the return trip. When you come to the mid-point of your journey, hug strongly its wings and you will see that he will disappear".

So it was that the woman prepared the letter and gave it in tears to her husband.

"Why are you so desperate?".

"Read the letter and you'll understand".

The gentleman picked it up and read it. Then he said, "do not cry. Tomorrow we will leave and you will see your beloved mother".

The next day the couple arrived bright and early to her parents' home.

"What are you doing here, my child?" the mother, who was in good health, asked at once.

"Hush, mother! Pretend to be sick and tell my husband you wanted to see me again in a hurry. In fact, I must tell you a terrible secret of great importance".

So it was that the daughter told her mother all that she had discovered.

The mother, before her daughter left once again, immediately gave her a rooster and prepared it for the journey.

The wife and the husband left.

When the carriage was in the middle of the journey, the woman took the rooster and squeezed his wings.

At that point the man disappeared and she was happily able to return to her home.

11. The Drool of the Mother Mermaid

Once upon a time in Gallura there was a king named Ingria.

He lived in a beautiful palace built out of granite, in front of a white and pink sandy beach.

In one of the halls there was a very large painting depicting a beautiful woman.

One day, a courtier named Brinaldhu told the king, "Your Majesty, did you know that my sister is *linta e pinta* (an exact copy) to the lady depicted in the portrait?".

"Really? Show her to me and you will be rewarded. But be careful, if she is not like this *pintura* (painting), I'll have your head cut off," said King Ingria.

The courtier, who was originally from Corsica, returned to his town in the midst of the mountains.

He immediately looked for his sister and told her, "do you know that King Ingria wants to see you? Prepare yourself so that I can take you to the castle".

"Bring your other sister too, so she can be the maid-of-honor" said their mother, indicating the *foster sister* who had been raised as mercy and nourished with her breasts.

When the three were on the ship going from Bonifàciu to the port of Lungoni, the foster sister threw the bride-to-be of the King Ingria into the waves of the Bocche (Mouths), because she was jealous of her sister's beauty and wanted to be the king's wife herself.

As soon as Mother Mermaid saw the girl fall into the sea, she lightly caught her and tied her foot with a strong but thin chain.

She then took her to a beach, not far from the king's palace, where the young girl would spend her days wandering around.

All of the pigeons of King Ingria's palace would also go to wander on the beach.

When the girl saw them she asked, "my beautiful Pigeons, do you have any news of my brother Brinaldhu?".

"Your brother is dead. The King cut his head and buried it under his throne," said one of the birds.

"*Cori meju e vidda mia* (my heart and my life)!" exclaimed with pain the girl, chained to the sea.

As the sky was getting dark and threatening, she began to weep and beat her body, while from her hair fell grains of wheat for the pigeons.

"*Sacra Curona meja* (my Sacred Crown)!" said one of the servants upon seeing the girl talking to the pigeons of the palace. He went to the king and said, "Your Majesty, if only you saw what I have seen with my own eyes and heard what I heard with my own ears."

"What the hell are you talking about?" said the king.

"A very pretty girl who can speak with the pigeons came out from the sea".

"Really?".

"*Eja* (Yes)".

"If this thing is not true, I'll have your head cut off. Tell me when the pigeons leave the palace and go to the sea shore again," concluded King Ingria, somewhat incredulously.

After some time, the valet called the king, "*Sacra Curona meja*! Majesty, hurry to see the pigeons who speak with the beautiful chained maiden, who came from the sea".

The girl, unhappy and in disbelief, was still asking the pigeons for news about her brother. The king, who had approached unnoticed, suddenly came forward and asked "What are you doing here? Who has chained you in this way?".

"The Mother Mermaid has tied me," said the girl, showing the chain linking a toe to the sea.

"How do we take it off?".

"I do not know. I will have to ask her," said the beautiful sister of the dead courtier, diving into the waves.

"As soon as the pigeons come back, let me know," the king ordered the servant.

Once she was deep in the sea, the girl asked the Mother Mermaid, "*Mamma Sirena meja,* how may this *cadenita* (chain) that is tied to my foot be cut off?".

"I will not tell you, because I know that you will cheat me," answered the mermaid, who was about to take a bit of drool that was coming from her mouth to put into a barrel.

"Please, Mother Mermaid, tell me, because I love you and would never betray you".

"It must be cut with a silver hammer forged by three blacksmiths".

"Tell me one more thing, *Mamma Sirena meja*, what do you need this drool for?".

"This drool is important because when I find a dead man I put their bones in place, then rub a little of drool over them and the person comes back".

"*Mamma Sirena meja*, could you stretch the chain just a little, please?", the charming girl asked and, before returning to the beach, managed to take a little of the magic drool.

As soon as she came up from the sea, the pigeons went at once to greet her.

The King was notified.

He approached the beauty in chains and immediately asked, "did you find out how to cut this chain?".

The girl told King Ingria what she had heard from the mermaid.

Wasting no time, the king had a hammer forged as had been instructed and, as soon as it was ready, he released the girl.

At one point Mother Mermaid pulled the chain to call the girl, but this was now empty.

"I've been cheated!" she cried sadly.

The girl, free at last, was brought to the palace.

There she exhumed the body of her brother who, thanks to the drool of the mermaid, rose.

After King Ingria had heard the whole story, he called the foster sister of the two.

He asked the beautiful girl to marry him.

"My Star, what should I do with this perfidious traitor? Shall I have her head cut off?".

"No," replied Brinaldhu's charming blood-sister, who was effectively identical to the lady depicted in the painting, "make her a nun and then lock her in a convent".

12. The Orcs and the Nuraghi

There was once a man who everyone called *Traidori* (Traitor) because he was considered a rogue.

The man lived in the time when there were still orcs in Sardinia.

These, due to their size, lived in the Nuraghi, which are the stone towers on the island, and frightened local people.

One day the king asked Traidori to bring him an ogre in exchange for a nice prize.

What did Traidori do?

He went to a large old *nuraghe* where an orc lived.

As soon as the giant saw him, he said, "I have finally found something to put in my mouth!".

But Traidori answered immediately, "wait, be patient. I came to see you because I've decided to give you two men to eat, but I need a trunk to bring them here to you".

"Really?" said the orc in disbelief, coming out from the imposing tower of stones. "Yes, it's all true. In fact I came just to build the trunk," said the man who had brought with him saw, axe, hammer and nails.

So, what did Traidori do next?

He began to chop wood and build the trunk.

When all that was needed was to add the top, Traidori told the ogre, "I'm done! I've made the trunk and the lid! Now all we need to do is one thing: try to get in to see if everything is fine. In the meantime I will try to secure the cover".

"All right," said the giant leaping into the trunk.

Once inside, Traidori said, "I will now put the lid on. You should check that there is no light coming in from the outside, so that the two men may not find a hole and run away".

"All right," said the orc, while Traidori started nailing the lid to the box.

Then he asked, "is there any light now that I have put the lid on?".

"Hey, look! There is a little light here," said the ogre, while the man expertly closed the trunk with the hammer and nails.

Once the box was well-sealed, Traidori took it to the king, who gave him a bag full of gold coins as a reward.

When the trunk was opened, the orc had already died.

Since then the orcs have permanently left the Nuraghi, because men had finally been able to defeat the giants.

Index